WHEN *the* WOODS HUM

JOANNE RYDER

Illustrated by

CATHERINE STOCK

Morrow Junior Books / New York

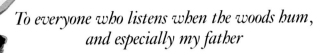

To everyone who listens when the woods hum,
and especially my father

J.R.

Inquiries should be addressed to
William Morrow and Company, Inc.,
105 Madison Avenue, New York, NY 10016.
Printed in Singapore at Tien Wah Press, 1991.
1 2 3 4 5 6 7 8 9 10
Library of Congress Cataloging-in-Publication Data
Ryder, Joanne.
When the woods hum / by Joanne Ryder; illustrated by Catherine Stock.
p. cm.
Summary: Jenny experiences the wonder of seeing and hearing the
woods fill up with humming cicadas, and seventeen years later she
returns with her young son to share that experience.
ISBN 0-688-07057-4 (trade).—ISBN 0-688-07058-2 (lib. bdg.)
[1. Cicada—Fiction.] I. Stock, Catherine, ill. II. Title.
PZ7.R959Wh 1991
[E]—dc20 90-37879 CIP AC

Author's Note

Almost every spring, in yards and woods scattered across the eastern United States, thousands—even millions—of red-eyed insects hum in the treetops. People look up and listen to a sound they have long forgotten or perhaps never heard before.

The insect hummers are periodical cicadas that have been living underground for either thirteen or seventeen years, quietly growing beneath our feet. Found only in North America, they are among the longest-living insects in the world. We realize they are near only when the nymphs emerge in vast numbers, becoming adult winged insects that hum and mate for a few short weeks.

The appearances of broods of periodical cicadas have been recorded for centuries. In 1634, the Pilgrims were amazed to hear their New England woods hum with these unfamiliar insects. Descendants of that brood of cicadas have emerged every seventeen years, as regular as clockwork. The twenty-first generation appeared in the spring of 1991, and the nymphs born then will live underground, feeding and growing, until 2008.

As our woodlands are cut down, the broods of periodical cicadas are fewer and smaller in number. But still, there are places where these unique insects grow unseen and suddenly appear, filling our woods with their songs of life.

Papa's path led through the old woods. It was a small path but wide enough for Papa and Jenny to walk under the trees, turning green with the first days of spring.

"Once, when I was young," Papa told Jenny, "I heard the woods hum."

"They hummed?" said Jenny.

"Um-hmm," said Papa, smiling. "They roared."

"I'd like to hear that," said Jenny.

"I think you will," said Papa. "The hummers are coming. They're coming up at last." And he pointed to a few tiny holes in the dark ground, leading to places Jenny could not see.

"Are they hiding?" asked Jenny.

"They're waiting," said Papa, "and it's almost time."

Jenny curled up on the yellow roses on her yellow bed, waiting for Papa to wish her good night.

"I have something for you," he said, and he brought her a round box, small and old. Inside was an insect with long glistening wings.

"What is it?" Jenny asked softly. She touched its fat black body, its orange wings shining in the lamplight.

"A cicada," Papa said. "One of the hummers from long ago. After it died, I kept it to remember that time. I've kept it for seventeen years."

"Seventeen years," Jenny whispered, and she put the old insect in her keeping place.

As spring settled in, the woods turned greener. Tiny leaves grew larger and danced in the breeze. In the treetops, hidden birds sang.

One evening, warmer than the rest, Papa called, "Come quickly, Jenny. The hummers are up."

Their flashlights made bright circles on the path through the dark woods. "Look at all the holes, Papa!" Jenny said.

There were thousands of holes under the trees now. Thousands of small wingless creepers were leaving their underground homes, climbing up tree trunks and clinging to branches.

Jenny watched a golden creeper swell and crack. "It's breaking," she called.

"It's splitting its old tight skin," said Papa.

Out of the golden skin crawled a soft white insect, its crumpled wings unfolding like petals in the dark.

Papa's light danced along the branches, where other creepers were changing, unfolding their new long wings.

"They look like flowers," said Jenny. Above her, the branches seemed filled with soft white flowers opening in the dark night.

The next morning, Jenny ran through the woods. Cicadas, no longer pale and soft, were testing their new wings. Here and there, a few dark flyers fluttered from branch to branch.

Thousands of tiny gold ghosts—the hard hollow skins of the creepers—lay on the ground. Jenny picked up a ghost skin, light and empty, and carried it home cupped in her hands.

"The cicadas are quiet," she told Papa. "Won't they hum now?"

"A few will start soon," he said. "But they need time to rest and get strong. They've made a big change. And more of them are coming up and they'll change, too. You'll hear them, all of them. Just wait."

brrrrrrr . . .

One sunny morning, the woods hummed. The humming grew louder and went on and on and on.

BRRRRRRR . . .

"They're here, Papa," Jenny called.

They ran together to the woods and stood in the bright spaces between the tall trees. Fat black insects flickered and danced above them, flew past them on shiny orange wings.

And the woods hummed with the sound of tiny vibrating drums.

"Oh, listen, Jenny," Papa shouted, louder than the *brrr*-ing drums. "The hummers are back at last."

One hummer landed on Jenny's arm and looked at her with ruby red eyes. Two tiny drums on his fat body quivered and trembled.

brrrrrrr . . .

"Why are they so noisy, Papa?" Jenny shouted.

"Because there are thousands and thousands," said Papa.

More and more hummers joined in, till the woods roared.

"What are they doing?" asked Jenny.

"They're calling," said Papa. "The males do the drumming and the females come find them. Then they can mate."

By suppertime, the woods grew quiet as the cicadas rested.
Papa sat on the porch, remembering the last time the
woods hummed, the spring he had pitched a
no-hitter.

"After we won," he told Jenny, "I flew home
on my bike with the woods roaring,
cheering all around me."

"How old were you, Papa?" asked Jenny.

"Just twelve," he said, smiling. "It's been a long time."

Day after day, male cicadas drummed and gathered in the treetops. Female cicadas flew to the trees, and there, on high sunny branches, they mated.

As Jenny watched, a female cicada slit a twig and laid rows of eggs inside it.

When spring turned to summer, the woods grew quiet. Here and there along the path, Jenny found a cicada, silent and still. "They're dying," she said to Papa. "They're all dying."

"I know," said Papa. "But the new ones will hatch soon."

And one hot day, they watched a young red-eyed creeper, small as an ant, run along its twig. It ran off the edge, tumbled down, and crawled inside a crack in the soft dark earth.

"It's gone," said Jenny. "What will it do?"

"Grow," said Papa. "It will find a tree root and stay close. It will suck juices from the root and grow."

When the days grew chilly, Jenny ran through the woods as red leaves fell, covering the path, covering the tiny cicadas underground. They would be hidden for a very long time.

"Seventeen years," she thought. "I wonder what I'll be like in seventeen years."

Seasons changed and years passed. Jenny grew taller, nearly as tall as Papa.

Underground, the little cicadas also grew, sucking the good juices from the tree roots, growing, then splitting their too-tight skins so they could grow some more.

One summer morning, Jenny walked down the path from the old house to be married in the bright space between the tall trees.

And in the spring, she brought her new son to see the old house and the woods.

"I named him Raymond, after you, Papa," she said.

Years passed and the woods changed, too. People came and cut trees and built homes. Some of the cicadas had no roots to feed them. Deep underground, they stopped growing and died.

But all through the years, Papa walked down his path, watching birds come and go, watching snows fall and melt.

Then one spring, he wrote Jenny a letter:
"Come soon if you can, and bring Ray. Your hummers are almost ready."

*   *   *

In the woods, a soft breeze tickled the new green leaves over Papa's head. And he turned as he heard two voices calling to him, "We're here. We're here."

"Are they up?" asked Ray. "Is it time?"

"Almost," said Papa, and he showed Ray a few tiny holes around the bushes and the trees, leading to dark places they couldn't see.

And that evening, when it grew dark, golden creepers dug up to the surface and peeked out of their holes. They climbed up the trees and shed their tight skins. Soft and white, they spread their new wings.

"Oh, Mama," said Ray. "They do look like flowers."

brrrrrrr . . .

High on a branch, a fat black insect drummed. Up on the hill,
Jenny opened her window to hear.

Brrrrrrr . . .

Ray sat on his bed, holding a round box and touching the old, shining one tucked inside.

BRRRRRRR . . .

"Get up, everybody," called Papa. "The hummers are back!"

They ran down the hill to the old woods filled with noise and insects flickering in the trees.

Jenny caught one on her sleeve. "Oh, I wondered about you," she said softly. "I wondered if you were growing, and if I'd ever see you again."

And she and Papa took Ray down the small path through the woods that hummed and roared with the sound of cicadas calling at last, calling once more.

Cicada Sketches

PERIODICAL CICADA
We see these ruby-eyed cicadas every 17 years. (In some areas, they appear every 13 years.) A large kind makes a steady hum, and a smaller kind has a louder ticking, buzzing call. We hear hundreds of thousands of them in late May and in June.

For Ray—I thought you might like these sketches of mine to remember our cicadas. Love, Grandpa

ANNUAL CICADA These greenish-winged cicadas live in our woods, too. We hear them more often because a smaller number become adults each summer. They appear in July and August.

All adults have wings!

Cicadas have 3 stages of life: egg, nymph, and adult.

NYMPH

EGG

LOBSTERLIKE FRONT CLAWS FOR DIGGING AND GRASPING

BEAKLIKE MOUTH SUCKS SAP

PERIODICAL ADULT FEMALE

A female has a hollow needlelike organ for laying up to 600 eggs.

Adults feed on sap from twigs. They cannot bite or sting.

EGG LAYER

PERIODICAL ADULT MALE

DRUMS

A male has two tiny drums, one on each side of his body. Muscles make these drums vibrate.

The sound a cicada makes is called chirring. Each kind of cicada chirrs its own song. It's great to hear them all!